S⚽CCER SQUAD

SQUAD

MISSING!

Bali Rai

Illustrated by Mike Phillips

RED FOX

SOCCER SQUAD: MISSING!
A RED FOX BOOK 978 1 862 30655 4

Published in Great Britain by Red Fox,
an imprint of Random House Children's Books
A Random House Group Company

This edition published 2008

1 3 5 7 9 10 8 6 4 2

The Random House Group Limited supports the Forest Stewardship Council (FSC),
the leading international forest certification organization. All our titles that are printed
on Greenpeace-approved FSC-certified paper carry the FSC logo. Our paper procurement
policy can be found at www.rbooks.co.uk/environment.

Set in 14/22pt Meta Normal

Red Fox Books are published by Random House Children's Books,
61–63 Uxbridge Road, London W5 5SA

www.kidsatrandomhouse.co.uk
www.rbooks.co.uk

Addresses for companies within The Random House Group Limited can be found at:
www.randomhouse.co.uk/offices.htm

THE RANDOM HOUSE GROUP Limited Reg. No. 954009

A CIP catalogue record for this book is available from the British Library.

Printed in the UK by CPI Bookmarque, Croydon, CR0 4TD

I heard Abs shout, 'Jason, one-two!' I looked up, saw him to my right and passed him the ball just before one of Langton's defenders reached me. Then, instead of standing still, I moved into the box, at an angle from Abs – just like our coaches had shown us. Abs waited and then side-footed the ball into my path. Suddenly I was free – one on one with the keeper! In my head I could hear the lad teasing me . . .

I waited for their keeper to move and then I smashed the ball with my left foot. It flew like an arrow and nearly burst the net!

1–0!

Read every book in this action-packed

football series:

STARTING ELEVEN

MISSING!

Coming soon:

STARS!

GLORY!

MISSING!

Chapter 1

Thursday

'Football is all about passion,' one of our coaches, Mr Turner, said to us. 'Passion, pride and playing for each other . . .'

We were sitting in our local youth club, going over why we'd lost two games out of two in the junior league and I was worried. My team, the Rushton Reds, was different from the others. We had girls playing for us. *Girls*.

'Are you listening to me, Jason?' Mr Turner asked me.

I nodded and shrugged at the same time. My mates were there with me: Dal, Chris and Abs, as well as the rest of the lads. *And* the girls . . .

'I think we need to practise defending,' said one of the girls, Lily. She's OK, but she's got a big mouth and she never stops talking.

'Thanks for that,' said our second coach, Mr James.

'Yes – we'll definitely do that,' said the third coach, an American lady called Miss Rice.

'And I think shooting too,' added Lily. 'I mean, how are we supposed to win if we don't score goals?'

'Yes, Lily,' replied Mr Turner, with a smile.

I turned to Abs and sighed.

'Stupid girl,' he whispered as Miss Rice stood up from her chair.

'Soccer is about team play,' she said. 'And

we just aren't playing as a team, y'all,'
Miss Rice added.

'*Football*, miss!' said Chris.

'*Potayto, potarto,*' replied Miss Rice in a
silly voice. 'You may call it football, but to
the rest of the world it's soccer . . . got it?'

Chris nodded.

'We're gonna get stuffed in every game,'
whispered Dal.

This time I shrugged. We didn't *have* to
lose the next game. It wasn't certain. We just
had to play better. But how were we going to
do that with girls in the team?

Me and my friends – Dal, Abs and Chris –
had joined the Rushton Reds, a new team,
at the beginning of the season. Abs and
Chris are wicked strikers, whilst Dal plays in
defence. I'm a midfielder. We'd been so
excited at making the squad and then
playing in the starting eleven. But that had

changed. And quickly too. Because of a freak wave of injuries to some of the other lads, we'd ended up having to play with girls in the team. And to make it worse, one of our coaches, Miss Rice, had told one of her friends about it. A friend who worked for the local TV station.

'It'll make great TV,' she'd explained to the team. 'They're going to come and watch a training session and maybe even a game. If they like what they see, they may make a film about you. You might all get to be interviewed too!'

'Will it be on proper telly, miss?' Dal had asked.

'If they go ahead and make the film,' Miss Rice had replied.

'Will we get money for it?' asked Abs. 'Like proper players?'

'Don't be silly, Abs,' Lily had told him.

'What's more sillier than girls playing

football?' he'd asked.

'You playing football,' one of the other girls, Parvy, had added.

'Or using odd phrases like "more sillier",' Lily had continued.

And now here we were – talking about how rubbish we'd been so far – and how we might end up on the telly. Great! If that went ahead, everyone I knew would find out. The Rushton Reds were going to be one big joke. Not only were we losing games, but we had girls playing too!

'We need to stop missing our chances,' Mr Turner said, getting back to the football.

Everyone nodded. Except for me and another player called Steven. We didn't nod because we'd both missed chances already. From the penalty spot! In the same game too – our second of the season! Which we had lost, just like we'd lost our first match.

'I'll take the penalties next time!' shouted Abs. 'I would have *buried* the two that *they* missed.' He nodded towards me and Steven.

'Now, now,' said Mr James. 'There's no need to pick on anyone. It's a team game, as Miss Rice has just told us.'

Abs pulled a face.

'And that's what we are going to concentrate on this evening,' Mr Turner told us. 'So go and get changed and we'll see you outside.'

I stood up and followed the rest of the lads to the changing room.

'Hey, Jason, now that the injured players are fit again we don't need the girls anyway,' Abs said as we walked in.

Dal shook his head. 'Four of the original squad have left already,' he reminded Abs.

It was true. After our first game, some of

the other boys hadn't come back. And there were even fewer after the second game.

'So it looks like we're stuck with the girls,' Dal added.

Chris opened a packet of peanuts and stuffed them all into his mouth. He's cool, Chris. He's always smiling or eating nuts. When he'd swallowed them he counted the number of players in the changing room.

'There's twelve of us – Steven, Byron, Leon, Corky, Ben, Pete, Ant and Gurinder plus us four. So even with the girls, including the new one, Gem, we've only got seventeen players,' he said.

'What happens if we get more injuries?' asked Abs.

'More girls probably,' I replied.

'That's not fair!' squealed Abs, sounding like he was five rather than ten years old.

'That's enough,' said Mr James, who'd

just walked into the changing room.
'Let's concentrate on the next game.'

'Yeah,' said Chris, with a grin. 'Stop
complaining like a baby, Abs, and listen.'

Abs gave Chris a glare but didn't say anything else.

Our next match was against another team
which was new to the league – just like ours.

They were called Langton Blues and they
hadn't won a game yet either. So I was
feeling confident.

'We're going to do something a little bit
different today,' Mr James told us. 'Now
hurry up and get changed . . .'

'What are we doing?' asked Dal.

'Dancing,' replied Mr James with a smile.

'*Dancing?*' I said. 'Why are we going
to be—?'

But Mr James had already left the room.

'This is getting stranger and stranger,' Dal
said to me.

'We'll be wearing skirts next,' added Abs. 'You wait and see.'

But we didn't really dance when the training session began. It just looked like we were. Mr Turner put us in pairs and got us to face each other. I was with Abs. The coach told us to put our arms out and our hands on each other's shoulders. Then he gave us a number. I was number one and Abs was number two. Each of the pairs was the same too.

'Now keep at arm's length,' instructed Mr Turner. 'When I shout your number, I want you to run forwards. Your partner will follow you. You must not let go of your partner's shoulders.'

I was confused. 'I don't get it, sir,' I complained.

'It's simple, Jason,' said Miss Rice. 'Each of you will lead the other. If we shout "one!" then it's your turn to run forwards and Abs will run backwards. When the whistle blows, you switch immediately and Abs runs forwards with you going backwards.'

I shrugged. 'That's about as clear as mud!' I told her.

'Don't be silly,' I heard Lily say. I turned my head and saw that she was behind me, with Parvy as her partner. 'Look – we'll show you.'

She started to run forwards and at the same time Parvy matched her stride for stride. Only Parvy was going backwards. After a few seconds Miss Rice blew her whistle and they switched. This time Parvy ran forwards and Lily matched her steps.

'It's all about coordination,' Mr James told us.

'And us girls have got it . . .' said Parvy.

'OK,' added Mr Turner, looking at me. 'Get ready. On my whistle, I want all the number ones to run forwards. Each time I blow on it, I want you to switch.'

I nodded at him.

'Go!' he shouted before blowing on his whistle.

I started to run forwards slowly and Abs tried to match my steps. But I'm taller than Abs and I've got longer legs so he couldn't keep up. After about ten steps he fell over in the mud.

'Come on, Abs, Jason!' shouted Miss Rice. 'It's easy!'

Abs complained, but got up and we started again. Then Mr Turner blew his whistle once more. This time I started to go backwards, but Abs didn't realize that we'd changed and we let go of each other's shoulders.

'Come on, lads!' Mr James said to us. 'Coordination . . .'

After a while we began to get it right.

'We're dancing,' Abs said to me. 'Like girls.'

'Just concentrate,' I told him.

'Skirts,' he said. 'I'm telling you!'

I was about to say something to him but he fell over again. I tried not to laugh, but I couldn't help it. Everyone else joined in too.

Chapter 2

Saturday

My mum gave me a lift to the game at
Langton Blues and when I got there Dal,
Chris and both their dads were already
there. Langton's home ground was at a
school called Brookside High which was
on the other side of the city. It was cold
and wet and the rain was getting down
the back of my hooded top. I walked over
to my mates and asked them if anyone else
from our team had arrived. Dal shook
his head.

'The girls are coming with Miss Rice,' he told me. 'I don't know about the rest of the lads . . .'

'Where's Abs?' I asked.

'His brother is bringing him,' replied Chris.

'I hope he stops moaning,' I said. 'He was going on and on at training . . .'

Chris nodded. 'He's like a baby,' he joked. 'I might get him some nappies.'

'I bet he'd even moan about them,' added Dal.

'I wonder if you can get Man U nappies,' continued Chris. 'We could get him some for his birthday.'

Abs is a Manchester United fan whereas I support Chelsea. Chris and Dal both like Liverpool. All four of us are always taking the mickey out of each other and Abs is the biggest culprit.

'What teams do the girls support?' I asked.

We had five girls in our squad – Lily, Parvy, Emma, Penny and Gem – and I didn't know too much about them. Lily was the loudest, followed by Parvy, but the rest of them were quite shy. Or that's what it seemed like to me.

'Lily likes Arsenal,' Dal told us.

'You *would* know that!' laughed Chris.

'What does that mean?' asked Dal, looking confused.

Chris smirked. 'Well, she *is* your girl-friend,' he said.

'No she *isn't!*' protested Dal. 'That's just her being stupid . . .'

'Well, I don't know who she supports,' I added, joining in with Chris. 'She doesn't tell *me* her secrets . . .'

Dal went red. 'She doesn't tell me any secrets,' he protested. 'She just told me who she supports at training last week . . .'

Chris looked at me and winked. 'You

mean, when you were both alone together?'

Dal went even redder. 'We were not alone together!' he shouted, loud enough for our parents, who were standing having a boring adult conversation, to hear.

'Everything OK, lads?' asked Chris's dad.

'Yeah, Dad,' said Chris, looking put out.

'OK,' replied his dad before turning back to my mum.

Everyone else turned up about ten minutes later and we went to get changed. When we got back out to the pitch the rain had got heavier. Within five minutes I was soaked. *And* worried about the outcome of the match. The coaches had decided to stick with the same team that had been beaten in our last game. We were standing in a huddle by the touchline and some of the players were complaining.

'I can't believe we are playing the same

team,' moaned Byron, one of our midfielders.

'Relax, lads,' Mr James told us. 'We only lost our first two games because of missed chances. Overall our play was great. We need to work on that today . . .'

'*Yeah*,' said Abs, who was usually the biggest moaner of the lot. 'Let's be positive, people!'

Mr James looked at Abs and smiled. 'Yes,' he agreed, 'let's be positive. Remember – pass and move – look for each other. Get the tackles in . . .'

We had Gurinder in goal with a back four of Leon, Dal, Steven, who was our captain, and Parvy. I was in the midfield with Byron and Lily to my right and Corky to the left. Up front were Abs and Chris. 4-4-2. Exactly the same team that had played our first two games.

On the bench were Gem, who is our other

goalkeeper, Ant, Pete, Ben and Emma. The only player in the squad not here today was a girl called Penny. She was away with her parents.

The girls went off to talk to Miss Rice as the rest of us took up position. Then the girls rejoined us and we were ready. I looked at the lads from Langton and some of them were wearing smirks. As soon as Abs touched the ball to Chris and the game began, their central midfielder started teasing me.

'You're getting stuffed!' he said to me. He was about my height with a piggy nose and freckles.

'Yeah, yeah!' I replied.

'You lot are rubbish,' the lad continued. 'Don't you feel ashamed playing with girls?'

'Oh, get lost!' I shouted at him as the ball made its way out to Parvy. She tried to control it but it slipped under her foot and went out for a throw-in.

'See?' said the lad.

I started to get really angry with him and before the throw-in was taken by Corky, I ran over to get ready to take the ball. I was going to show him!

Corky saw me and threw me the ball. I turned with it and looked up. There was space down the left wing so I ran down the channel with the ball. From my right I could see the mouthy lad coming in to tackle me so I waited until he was close and then switched inside. My move left him flat on his feet and I was bearing down towards the goal.

I heard Abs shout, 'Jason, one-two!' I looked up, saw him to my right and passed him the ball just before one of Langton's defenders reached me. Then, instead of standing still, I moved into the box, at an

angle from Abs – just like our coaches had shown us. Abs waited and then side-footed the ball into my path. Suddenly I was free – one on one with the keeper! In my head I could hear the lad teasing me . . .

I waited for their keeper to move and then I smashed the ball with my left foot. It flew like an arrow and nearly burst the net!

1–0!

The rest of the Rushton Reds jumped on me as I yelled 'GOAAAAALLLL!' at the top of my voice.

When I'd calmed down I heard Miss Rice shouting at me. 'Get back in position!' she told me. 'Concentrate . . .'

I jogged back to midfield and waited for the restart. Immediately the mouthy lad with the freckles picked up the ball and slipped past Corky and Lily with a drop of his left shoulder. He was good. The ball seemed to stick to his feet and as I moved in to make a tackle, he spun round and played the ball out to the right wing.

The boy who took the ball was tall with really skinny legs and bright-red hair. He looked up and saw Parvy. Then he ran right at her. I looked at Corky and shouted at him to back her up. Then I spotted another Langton midfielder making his way towards our penalty area.

Danger!

I sprinted to catch up with him. As I did that, the red-haired winger dribbled the ball past Parvy and Corky and was into our box. I saw Dal move across to challenge him but the Langton striker played the ball in behind our defenders and the player I was tracking turned it into the net just a split second before I could reach him.

It was 1–1.

'NO!!!!!!!!!!!!' I heard Abs and Chris shout together.

The game wasn't even five minutes old and we'd scored one and let one in. On the touchline Mr James wore a face like thunder and Mr Turner was bright-red with anger. Only Miss Rice seemed relaxed. As we retook our positions for the kickoff, she said a few words to Byron and Lily. I don't know what she said to them, but from the moment the ball was kicked, Byron went and man-marked the mouthy lad with the freckles. That left me with the fast player who had scored the equalizer. He was short and stocky with fat legs and his whole body looked like a rectangle. But he was quick. As he moved to receive the ball again, I ran across to him and he quickly passed the ball on.

'You look like SpongeBob SquarePants,' I said to him.

He turned to me and grinned. 'At least I'm not playing with the Bratz team,' he replied.

'Who's your substitute – Barbie?'

I wanted to say something back to him, but I didn't get a chance. Instead, I saw Byron beat the freckled lad and pass the ball out to Lily. She took it in her stride and then did about three step-overs as she ran at Langton's left back. I hate to admit it but Lily was really good at step-overs. Instead of taking their back on, though, she passed the ball into the centre where Abs took it up. He took on two defenders and created an opening.

I could see Chris running, unmarked, into space. He was screaming for the ball but Abs only had one thing on his mind. He turned back inside the defenders he had already beaten and tried to slot the ball into the net. But their keeper was alert to the danger and he scooped the ball up and held it safely to his chest.

'Abs!' shouted Chris. 'I was totally unmarked . . . !'

'Sorry,' Abs replied, holding up his hands and looking sheepish.

I watched the Blues' keeper throw the ball to his right back. The player passed it on to the red-haired winger, who went on another run. This time, though, he tried to be too clever. As Parvy came in, he attempted to flick the ball over her but didn't succeed. Parvy saw what he was trying and she won the ball and passed it square to Corky.

Langton's winger looked gutted and he said something to Parvy.

Parvy turned to him and smiled. 'Tackled by a girl,' she joked.

'Get lost, you stupid *girlie*!' the lad replied.

Suddenly the whistle was blown and the ref went over to the lad.

'No more of that, son!' he warned.

'Yessir . . .' replied the lad, looking really embarrassed.

From the sidelines I heard my mum screaming.

'YOU GO, GIRL!' she shouted.

I could feel myself going red, but then Dal's and Chris's dads joined in too.

'COME ON, YOU REDS! COME ON, YOU REDS!'

Chapter 3

At half-time the score was still 1–1 and Mr Turner told us that he was pleased with us, despite the fact that we'd conceded such a quick equalizer.

'I keep telling you,' he said. 'All teams are at their most vulnerable when they've just scored. That's why you've *got* to concentrate *twice* as hard when you score – got it?'

We nodded at him.

'And let's get the ball moving too, y'all,' added Miss Rice. 'Little triangles. Pass the ball and then move. Don't stand still. Give your team-mates an option . . .'

Again everyone nodded.

'Right, let's get out there and get our first points of the season,' said Mr James. 'Teamwork, effort, commitment. Come on, Reds!'

We walked back out onto the muddy pitch as the clouds broke again and it began to pour down. I looked over to the sidelines and saw my mum standing there, totally drenched but smiling with it. She blew me a kiss. Parents can be *so* embarrassing. I kind of nodded back and then took up my position. Lily came and stood next to me.

'Your mum is really pretty,' she told me.

'Shut up,' I said, because I didn't know what else to say.

'I mean it, Jason,' she insisted. 'She always wears really nice clothes. How come your dad never comes too?'

I shrugged. 'There's just me and Mum,' I told her.

Lily's face dropped. 'Oh,' she said. 'I didn't mean to . . .'

''S OK,' I told her. 'I know . . .'

She smiled at me. 'Pass me the ball more this half,' she said.

'Why?' I asked jokingly. 'You going to score the winner?'

Lily nodded as Abs and Chris walked over.

'I'm going to *ninja* their left back,' she told us, before making a squealing sound. *'YEEEEAH!'*

'What's up with you?' asked Abs. 'You feeling *ill* or something?'

'Just showing Jason what I'm going to do to their left back,' she said with a grin.

Dal joined us too.

'Hello, my dear,' Lily said to him, making him squirm. 'I was just telling your friends about how lovely you are . . .'

'Er . . .' began Dal.

'She said she was going to *ninja* their player,' I said to him.

'What does *that* mean?' asked Chris, getting confused, as Parvy walked up too.

'It means she's going to teach him to respect the *skills*,' said Parvy.

'Eh???' I asked.

'Just watch and learn, mere mortal,' replied Parvy. 'They only teach the way of the soccer *ninja* to *girls*.'

I looked at Chris, who shrugged. 'Must be some sort of USA thing,' he said. 'Because I do not have a clue what she just said to us. She might as well have spoken in *Teletubbese* . . .'

'Man – you lot are just *weird*,' said Abs. '*All* of you!'

Thankfully the referee told us to get ready for kickoff at that precise moment. Before Lily and Parvy could talk more nonsense and

Chris could attempt to explain what *'Teletubbese'* actually meant!

Langton got hold of the ball straight away and for the next ten minutes we seemed to be chasing shadows. Every time one of our players tried to get the ball they passed it on. After a while I started to get really frustrated and I decided that I was going to get hold of the ball.

I got my chance almost immediately when the lad with the freckles, who was called Luke, tried to run past me with the ball. Remembering what Mr James had said to me about timing my tackles, I watched and waited and then, just as Luke went to shimmy past, I stuck out my left foot and the ball broke free. I gathered it with my right foot and played it across the middle of the pitch to Corky. Corky stopped the ball and then played it on to Abs, who turned and ran at the goal. There were two defenders in front of him and this time he wasn't greedy. Instead of shooting at goal, he slipped the ball inside to Chris.

Chris saw a chance and tried to hit a low shot into the net, but one of Langton's defenders got in the way and the ball hit his left shin. I watched as it bounced out to Lily. I was running for the box now, ready to take the ball.

'LILY – SQUARE IT!' I shouted.

But she didn't listen. Instead she faced up to her defender and waited for him to go for the ball. When he did, she stepped across the ball and lifted it up into the air in one movement. From the sidelines I heard our parents and coaches cheering. Lily controlled the ball with her left foot and then lashed at it with her right.

It was heading straight at the keeper!

He moved to stop the shot, but at the last minute the ball seemed to swerve in the air.

It was like some kind of magic trick and it wrong-footed their goalie. His face dropped as he realized that he wasn't in the right position. Everything seemed to turn to slow motion. The keeper tried to reach the shot but he couldn't. It just evaded his fingertips. I froze to the spot as a low, moaning, cheering sound broke. The ball was in the back of the net.

2–1. And Lily was the goal-scorer!

The cheer brought the game back into focus and I ran over to Lily to congratulate her. But she was already being mobbed by the other players. Our parents were cheering and whooping with delight. I turned to see Luke looking ashen-faced.

'That's Barbie!' I told him with a grin, before taking my turn to congratulate Lily. Maybe things weren't going to be as bad as we had thought. Not only could Lily play a bit – she was *good*.

We held out for ten more minutes and then disaster struck.

Langton's red-haired winger found himself on the left this time, facing Leon. He had the ball at his feet and was running into space. As he entered our penalty area, Leon managed to tackle him but only for the loose ball to fall to Luke. He swept it into his stride and skipped a challenge from Dal, only to be faced with Gurinder.

But Gurinder got it all wrong. He didn't wait for the shot or try to smother the ball. Instead he lunged at Luke with his feet, totally missed the ball and brought him down.

Even though I knew it was coming, when the ref blew his whistle for a penalty, I was in shock. Surely we weren't going to let another lead slip?

As we trudged back to the edge of the box, Langton's captain – a smarmy-looking boy who they called Beggsy – placed the ball on the penalty spot. He turned and walked back eight paces and then turned again. He was facing the ball, facing Gurinder and facing the goal. He waited for the ref to blow his whistle – and then he ran at the ball and smashed it home with his right foot. Gurinder went the wrong way and we were back to where we'd begun.

2–2!

Langton went crazy, jumping up and down and teasing us with shouts of 'girls team'.

Even some of their parents joined in and I started to get really mad. I ran and grabbed the ball from Gurinder and sprinted back to the centre circle.

'Come on, Reds!' I shouted to my team-mates. 'Not again!'

But I had to wait for a few more minutes

before I could restart the game. The Langton players were still celebrating and a couple of them were pointing at Lily and laughing. She sidled over to me with Dal in tow.

'My husband and I have a plan, Jason,' she told me.

'I'm not your husband!' protested Dal.

'Oh, do be quiet and listen,' demanded Lily before turning to me. 'When you get the ball,' she told me, 'try and look for me on the wing. Once I get it, run into the box and I'll cross for you. I'm good at crosses. I'll put it right at your feet . . .'

I nodded, but I wasn't sure about her boast. I looked at Dal, who shrugged.

'And you, Dal,' continued Lily, 'you make sure that his marker – that ugly boy with the freckles – is busy. OK, hubby dearest?'

Dal shrugged again and went red.

'What are you trying to do?' I asked.

'Get you into their box with a clear

goal-scoring opportunity,' she replied. 'What do you think?'

'But what if you can't get the ball to me?' I added.

Lily pulled a face. 'Just get the ball to me and get into the box, OK?' she demanded.

I nodded.

It took me five minutes to even get the opportunity to pass Lily the ball, and then she couldn't do anything with it because she was surrounded by Langton players. Instead she sent it back to me and I played it on to Steven.

Steven looked up and saw Corky in space so he passed it on too. Corky ran with the ball past two Langton players and then squared to Byron. By this point I had run into the opposition half and was closing on their last line of defenders. I spotted Lily standing right out on the right-hand touchline. Maybe she was about to get her wish.

I called for the ball and Byron slid it at me. It was a hard and fast pass but I took it well and turned. Lily made her move, darting behind their left back, and I played the ball into the space she was running into.

I turned and ran for Langton's area, hoping that she would be able to get the ball back to me. I looked all around me but there was no one tracking my run. I was on my own and clear. Lily looked up, stepped over the ball again and then played it right in front of me.

I could see the ball approaching and I glanced at their goal. Just *four* minutes left of the game and only the keeper to beat. There was no other player near me. Making up my mind to shoot with my right foot, I adjusted my feet and went to strike the ball. But just before I could make contact, I felt my legs give way . . .

'PENALTY!' I heard the ref shout as I went down.

I rolled over and watched the Langton players going mad. They were protesting about the decision. Then I saw Lily standing over me, smiling. Byron and Dal were with her.

'Nice one!' said Dal. 'We did it.'

I got up and saw that Abs had taken the ball from Steven. He walked to the spot and placed it. I knew he'd score. I just *knew* it. And then we'd have our first victory of the season.

I watched calmly as Abs turned and walked back to his starting position. Then he looked at me and winked. I smiled back.

Abs waited for the ref to signal he was ready and then he stepped up, taking a diagonal run at the ball. He lifted his right foot and made contact . . . and missed, skying the ball high over the goal!

All around me Langton players started laughing. Abs put his head in his hands and sank to his knees.

'OH NO!' I cried out. *Another* missed penalty. Could no one in our team hit the net from the penalty spot . . . ?

Chapter 4

Tuesday

Tuesday was training night and we went through what had happened against Langton Blues. Mr Turner wasn't there. Instead we had Mr James and Miss Rice taking the session. And Miss Rice was urging us to think about how well we'd played.

'You were great, mostly,' she told us. 'Like a real team. You even passed the ball to each other . . .'

'We still didn't win, miss,' complained Dal. 'We're always the best at school – why can't we be the best in the league too?'

'Ah, but we will be the best if we continue to play like that,' Mr James said, holding a clipboard with lots of papers attached to it. 'And Dal, we got the point from the draw, remember.'

'Mr James?' asked Chris.

'Yes, son?'

Chris looked at me before he spoke. He looked unsure of what he was about to say. But in the end he spoke anyway.

'My brother plays for a team like ours and—'

'Does he want to join?' asked Mr James, doing something that adults tell us kids not to do but do themselves all the time. Interrupt when we're talking!

'No – he's too old, but he doesn't have to call his coach "sir" or "miss". Why do we have to?'

The entire squad gasped and looked at

Chris. It was as though he'd just sprouted a new head. We were shocked. Mr James looked at Miss Rice and they burst into laughter. When they'd calmed down, Miss Rice replied.

'We were talking about that the other week,' she told us. 'From the first training session all of you called us "sir" and "miss". We just thought you were all extra-polite.'

'Does that mean we don't have to?' asked Abs.

Mr James nodded. 'Not if you don't want to. I'm quite happy for you to call me Ian . . . and I'm sure Wendy would love it if you—'

'Wendy?' asked one of the girls, Gem. 'Like in *Peter Pan*.'

Miss Rice grinned. 'Exactly like *Peter Pan*,' she said. 'I can even fly . . .'

Most of us laughed or smirked at what Miss Rice had just said, but Gurinder – the first-choice keeper – can be a bit dim at times. He looked at Miss Rice and asked her how long it took to learn to fly.

'You fool!' shouted Abs. 'She can't really fly . . . can you . . . er . . . Wendy?'

'Only when I really have to, people,' Wendy replied.

'So what's Mr Turner's name?' I asked.

'Steve,' Wendy told us.

'That's so cool,' said Abs. 'Now it won't be like being at school when we play . . .'

Wendy and Ian gave him a funny look.

'I guess that'll be the lack of maths lessons,' suggested Ian.

Abs shrugged. 'Whatever,' he said.

Wendy told us to go and get changed, but Ian stopped her.

'We nearly forgot,' he said, pulling some of the paper off his clipboard. 'As our next game against Rockwell Rangers isn't for two weeks, we've arranged a special team-building exercise this Saturday . . .'

I looked at Dal and Chris. Chris's face was beaming with a big, broad grin.

'Like a trip?' he asked excitedly.

'Exactly that,' added Wendy. 'So we've got some notes for your parents. You will need their permission to come along and we'll also need at least two parents to come too.'

'So can you check with them when you get in later?' continued Ian. 'And let us know by Thursday. Your parents have our phone numbers.'

Dal's face fell a bit. 'What if none of our parents can make it?' he asked.

'Then it may be difficult to arrange but we'll see . . .' replied Ian.

'Why – where are we going?' asked Lily.

'To the moon,' joked Abs.

'Ahh!' replied Parvy, defending her friend. 'Look at that – the little boy tried to make a joke.'

The rest of the squad burst into laughter

and Abs scowled, but not for long. I think he was getting used to having the girls around after the weekend. Especially after Lily's brilliant goal. Not that he'd admit it.

'OK, OK,' said Wendy. 'Cool it! We were going to take you on a tour of Wembley but that fell through . . .'

'OHHHH!!!!!' we all said together.

'But,' she added, holding up her hand to stop us moaning, 'we will be doing that later in the season – as a reward – if you do well . . .'

'YEAAHHHHHHHHHHH!'

'Shut it!' shouted Ian.

As we calmed down, I asked where we were going instead.

'Paintballing,' replied Ian. 'A game of strategy and team—'

Only we didn't let him finish. Instead we all went crazy with excitement. It took ages for us to calm down. When we had, Wendy told us to go and get changed.

'Are we dancing again, miss?' asked Abs.

'Call me Wendy,' she said with a smile.

'And no, we're not dancing, although I could arrange it just for you if you'd like?'

'No thanks,' replied Abs.

'Didn't think so,' she added.

Dal's dad gave me, Abs and Chris a lift home too after training and we were all really excited about going paintballing.

'I'm gonna splat you all!' boasted Abs.

'Not if we're on the same team,' I told him.

'Oh yeah,' he said.

'What's this?' asked Dal's dad.

'Paintballing,' Dal told him. 'The coaches are taking us at the weekend. I've got a form for you to sign because we're too young or something . . .'

'Oh – OK,' replied his dad.

'And they need some parents to come too, Mr Singh,' I added. 'Will you do it?'

'This weekend, Jason?' asked Dal's dad.

For a second I was disappointed. When my mum doesn't want to do something I ask her to, she always replies like Mr Singh did. But then he surprised us.

'Yes – I don't see why not,' he said.

'Nice one, Dad!' beamed Dal.

'I've not been paintballing for years . . .'

'My dad'll do it!' added Chris.

'And mine!' said Abs. 'I'm sure he will want to.'

Dal's dad looked in his rear-view mirror at me. 'Ask your mum too, Jason,' he said to me. 'I'm sure she'd love to join us.'

I hadn't thought about asking my mum. I had just assumed that she wouldn't want to come along.

'I'll ask her when I get in,' I said. 'But she might be working.'

My mum works in an office and she does long hours sometimes. And I wasn't sure that I wanted her to come either. She'd probably want to wear high heels or something. She was great, but sometimes she could be a bit embarrassing too.

'We could have girls versus boys!' said Abs excitedly.

'You just fancy them,' joked Chris. 'That's why you're always having a go at Lily.'

'No!' complained Abs. 'And anyway, she's Dal's girlfriend.'

'No, she isn't,' moaned Dal.

'Oh, really?' asked Mr Singh. 'Is there something I should know, Dal?'

Dal's face dropped. 'No, Dad. Honest!'

Mr Singh winked at me in the mirror. 'Oh, chill out, kid – I was only joking,' he replied.

This time Dal looked embarrassed.

'Dad – can you please not use words like that?' he asked.

I smiled. Maybe my mum wasn't the only embarrassing parent in the world after all.

Chapter 5

Saturday

We got to paintballing at midday. Steve Turner had driven some of us in a minibus which he'd borrowed from a friend. The rest of the squad came with parents. Everyone in the squad turned up, along with about ten parents, including my mum. She was busy talking to Lily's mum, who had also come along. They were talking about nails and other girl things and I was glad to get away. I was standing with Dal and Abs, waiting to get started. But Wendy and Ian were still on their way and we had a bit of time to kill.

'We're gonna stuff Bolton,' said Abs, talking about Man United.

Dal shook his head. 'No you're not,' he replied. 'They're too good for you lot . . .'

'Rubbish,' said Abs.

'Yeah – just like your team,' added Dal.

I stayed out of the conversation because my team, Chelsea, weren't playing until Sunday. Instead, I was looking around. The paintballing place was huge. We were standing in a gravel car park, at the entrance to some woods. In front of us was a club-house-type place where we had registered. It was built of wood and had small windows. Next to it was a shop which sold things like paintball guns and other stuff, and next to that a small café, where most of the parents had gone straight away. Behind the buildings were the woods, with big old trees that looked dark and spooky. The course itself

was in there and I noticed that there were a
few maps pinned to posts which were dug
into the ground by the clubhouse.

'I'm going to look at the maps,' I said,
pointing to one.

Abs and Dal just grunted at me and went on
arguing about Liverpool and Man U. I shook
my head and walked over to one of the maps.
It showed a narrow pathway which ran in a

random pattern all around the course. There were two bases marked on it too, either side of a stream which had only four bridges shown across it. The bases were coloured red and blue. Also marked were an assault course area and five sets of sniper huts. These seemed to be directly opposite each other, which meant that they were going to be difficult to get past without getting hit. There were also thickets of trees marked all along the pathway, and beyond them, areas marked out of bounds. It looked great!

'I *love* paintballing,' I heard someone say.

I turned to see Penny, Gem and Emma standing behind me, smiling. It was Penny who had spoken. I didn't know what to say so I smiled and asked a stupid question.

'Have you been before?' I said. 'I thought Mr Turner said we were too young normally, so this was a day arranged just for us.'

Penny smiled at me. 'Well, they must do it for special groups, 'cause I went to a centre just like this one last year and I loved it! So yeah, I have been before – that's why I *like* it,' she replied.

'Oh, OK,' I said.

'I hope it's girls versus boys,' said Emma. 'We'll beat you easily . . .'

I shrugged. 'That's what Abs keeps saying – about boys v girls,' I explained.

'He doesn't like us, does he?' said Gem.

I shrugged again. 'He's just a bit funny about you playing for the team,' I replied. 'We didn't know that there'd be girls playing when we joined up so it was like a shock . . .'

Gem nodded and smiled at me. 'We don't like Abs,' she said, like she was talking for all of the girls.

'He's OK,' I said. I didn't want them to not like my mate. Abs could be silly sometimes, but he was a great friend.

'He's always having a go at us,' added Penny. 'Even after Lily scored that brilliant goal in the last game.'

Just then Byron, Ben and Leon turned up.

'What you doing, Jason?' asked Leon.

'Nothing,' I replied. 'Just looking at a map of the course.'

'It's going to be wicked!' said Byron with a huge grin.

'Yeah!' added Emma. 'Especially if it's boys versus girls . . .'

Ben shook his head. 'I asked Steve Turner and he said it won't be. They've already decided on the teams.'

'Have they?' I asked.

Ben nodded. 'All the defenders and the goalkeepers on one side and the midfielders on the other. The strikers are going to draw straws and the parents are going to join in too,' he told us.

Straight away I wondered if my mum would be on my side. I hoped not. That would so lame. But then I thought about how the teams would be split and I realized that I'd be on a different team from Dal.

'I can't wait,' said Gem. 'Let's go and see if we can get ready . . .'

'Ready for what?' I asked.

Gem smiled at me, but it was a nice smile. She wasn't teasing me. 'Mr Turner told us all about it on our way here,' she said. 'You get given overalls to wear and safety goggles and hats and things.'

I'd come with Dal in his dad's car with my mum so I didn't know anything about it.

'Oh,' I replied.

'That way we won't get paint in our eyes,' Gem explained.

'Or our hair,' added Emma. 'That would just be soooo horrible.'

I heard cars pull into the car park and saw Chris and his dad get out of one and Ian and Wendy get out of another.

'That's everyone then,' said Byron. 'Let's have some fun!'

We were split into two teams: Red and Blue. I was on the Red team and thankfully my mum wasn't, although I would have to shoot at her now. Instead I had Corky, Lily, Byron and Chris with me as well as Ant, Penny and

Emma. The adult Reds included Lily's mum and Dal's dad. After we'd been given our clothing and safety equipment we were taken off by one of the instructors, who showed us how to use the paint guns correctly. Once that was done we were led to the starting area, and I wondered what my mum would do if I got her with a paint ball. Knowing her she'd probably moan about having her hair out of place!

When we got there the Blue team had already gone. The lead instructor, who was called Gavin, told us why.

'The Blue base is located on the other side of the stream,' he said, pointing to a large version of the map I'd looked at earlier.

'What does that mean?' asked Lily.

'It means that their base is further away so they get a ten-minute head start on you lot,' replied Gavin. 'Once they're nearly there, I'll lead you to your base.'

'And then what happens?' I asked.

'Once both teams are at base, I'll tell my colleague that we're ready to start,' said Gavin.

He held up a walkie-talkie and showed it to us.

'The object of the game is simple. You need to take control of the enemy's base whilst also defending your own. To take their base you must clear it of any opponents and raise your own flag above it. The first team to do so *and* make it out of the course wins.'

I looked at Chris and saw that he was confused.

'But what if we all get hit by paint balls?' he asked.

'Then you lose,' replied Gavin. 'A minimum of *two* players *must* cross the finishing line untouched.'

'But what if all of us get hit, including all the Blue team too?' Chris added.

'Then it's a stalemate,' said Gavin. 'But that won't happen because I'm on your side and I've never been hit . . .'

He grinned at us proudly as Emma whispered, 'Bighead.'

'Can we shoot at our own team?' she asked.

Gavin gave her a funny look. 'Why would you want to do that, young lady?' he asked.

'In case one of them annoys me,' she replied as me and Chris tried not to grin too obviously.

'Oh,' said Gavin. 'Well, I've never seen that happen, but if you do hit one of your own team then it counts the same as a hit from the enemy.'

Dal's dad put up his hand to ask a question.

'Yes, mate?' asked Gavin.

'How many times can you get hit? Only when I last played, we—'

Gavin interrupted him. 'Oh – I nearly forgot to tell you. You are allowed two hits before you get a time-out. The time-out is ten minutes and then you're back on. But if you have more than *three* time-outs, then that's your game over – understood?'

'And then what do we do?' asked Emma.

'Then you make your way round the main path and out of the course . . . and hopefully stop asking so many questions.'

Gavin smiled at the rest of us, thinking we'd laugh at his little joke, but we didn't. We just stood and stared at him.

'He's a right idiot!' Chris whispered to me.

'I know. And I think Emma is going to get him,' I replied.

'Hope so,' said Chris.

Gavin said something into his walkie-talkie and then he told us it was time to go.

'Remember,' he said. 'It's about team-work. That's the only way to win.'

As he said it, Ian and Wendy joined us.

'Are you playing too, miss?' asked Chris.

'You betcha!' replied Wendy. 'Come on, Reds! And I've told you – call me Wendy.'

She smiled at Chris as Gavin told us to follow him.

'Stay close,' he warned. 'People do go missing in there . . .'

We should have listened to what he said, but we didn't. And we were going to pay for it . . .

Chapter 6

Our base was a large wooden cabin raised up on stilts to the front and resting against a steep bank to the back. In front of it ran the stream, which didn't seem too deep but was really wide. Once inside Gavin told us that we needed to split up.

'One unit to protect the base and another to attack the enemy.'

Emma and Lily both pulled faces.

'Were you in the *army*, Gavin?' asked Lily.

'Er . . . no,' he replied. 'Why?'

'Oh, nothing,' said Lily with a yawn. 'I just thought from the way you were talking that . . . oh, never mind.'

I gave Chris a nudge. 'They're messing him about,' I told him.

Chris nodded. 'He's a fool!' he whispered back. 'He deserves it.'

Gavin told us to decide amongst ourselves who was going to join which unit.

'I think it should be me, Chris, Jason and Emma!' shouted Lily. 'On the attack!'

'*Lily!* Stop being so demanding,' ordered Lily's mum.

'But I was only saying—' began Lily.

'I know, darling, but let someone else speak for a change,' said Lily's mum.

'Oh, Mum!' replied Lily, looking sheepish.

Gavin grinned. 'You've got five minutes to sort yourselves out,' he told us. 'And then I'll radio my colleague and we'll start . . .'

In the end Lily got her way about the attack unit. Joining the people she'd asked for were Wendy and Dal's dad. Everyone else stayed at base. Before we left, Gavin gave us a map of the course and some red stickers.

'Stick them to trees along the way so that you don't go in circles,' he told us.

'OK,' I nodded, taking them from him. 'But how are we going to know what you're doing?'

'Easy,' he said, grinning again.

He pulled the backpack he was wearing from his shoulders and produced two walkie-talkies. He handed one to Dal's dad and the other to Chris.

'The frequency is set to channel two,' he said. 'Don't change it.'

Chris nodded. 'No way, José,' he promised. 'What channel is the Blue team on?'

'Four,' replied Gavin. 'Right – get going and remember the plan. You take their base and then come back for us. If you need help, radio in and we'll send some. And work together, team!'

Once we were on the ground, I asked Dal's dad what we should do because he'd been paintballing before.

'I don't know, Jason,' he admitted. 'Every time I've ever been we just shoot at anyone. There's never been any of this war games stuff.'

'Oh,' I said, feeling a bit disappointed.

'Firstly,' said Wendy, 'we need to check out the map and work out the direction of their base. Then we move towards it . . .'

'Good idea, miss!' said Emma, getting excited.

'*Wendy!*' replied Miss Rice. 'For Pete's sake . . .'

'Who's *Pete*?' asked a confused-looking Chris.

'It's just an expression,' Wendy told him.

Chris grinned. 'Can we shoot Gavin?' he asked.

'I was going to ask that!' said Emma. 'Can we, *please????*'

Wendy smiled and looked at Dal's dad.

'Whaddya think, Mr Singh?'

'I think it's a great idea,' he said. 'But after we get back . . .'

'YES!!!!!!!!' said Chris and Lily together.

'He's *soooo* annoying,' added Emma.

'OK, Red Unit – move out!' shouted Wendy. 'Let's go kick some butt!'

According to Mr Singh, the Blue team base was to the north-west of our position, with the stream ahead of us. So we decided to head west, following the stream until we reached a bridge. Very quickly we found ourselves obstructed by huge trees. Wendy motioned for us to follow her into a thicket, which was dark and dense.

'Be careful,' she told us. 'It's wet under-foot . . .'

It had been raining during the morning and in places the ground was slippery with mud. I pushed some branches out of my face and looked around for any danger. But we were OK. There was no sign of the Blue team.

'It's horrible in here!' moaned Lily.

'Oh, shut up!' said Emma. 'It's fun.'

Chris tapped me on the shoulder from behind. I turned round to see him holding a beetle between his thumb and forefinger.

'Where'd you get that?' I asked.

'Fell on my head,' he replied. 'Shall I put it down Emma's back?'

I shook my head. 'We're supposed to be paying close attention,' I reminded him. 'If she screams, the Blues will know where we are.'

'So?' Chris shrugged. 'If they come for us, we'll blast them!'

Before I could say anything else he walked up behind Emma and dropped the beetle down the back of her protective suit. But if he'd been expecting her to react, he got a real shock. Emma turned round and laughed at him. Then without warning, she showed Chris the big, hairy caterpillar she was holding in her left hand. Chris shrieked like a little girl and stepped backwards.

'You girl!' shouted Lily.

'No!' protested Chris. 'I thought it was something else . . . like a . . . er . . . stick!'

Emma grinned. 'Big boy's blouse!' she said.

'Don't you mean girl's blouse?' I asked.

'No,' she told me. 'I *mean* boy's!'

'SSSSHHHHHHHHHHH!!!!!!!!!!!!!!!!!!'

It was Wendy and Mr Singh. We shut up and turned to them. Wendy was trying to point out something to our left. I looked around but I couldn't see anything. Then I turned right, towards where Mr Singh was pointing but there was nothing there either.

'What's going on?' whispered Lily.

'Blue team,' replied Mr Singh. 'Just beyond that line of trees. They must have taken the bridge we were going to cross . . .'

Wendy motioned for us to get down. She crouched to the floor and we followed suit. Suddenly a whooshing sound flashed overhead. Then another and another!

SPLAT!!!!!!!!!!!!!!!!

Blue paint slid down the tree trunk right next to my head.

'DUCK, YOU SUCKERS!!!!!!!!!!!!!!!!' someone shouted. Someone who sounded just like Abs.

'They've found us!' shouted Chris. 'Let's get out of here!'

'WAIT!' demanded Mr Singh. 'They can't

all be here. Probably only two of them. Let's try and circle them and get to the bridge.'

He pointed at me, Lily and Wendy and then gestured with his fingers for us to go left. Then he took the others right.

WHOOSH! SPLAT!!!!!!!!!!!!!! More blue paint balls zipped through the air until they smacked against tree bark. I ducked again.

'They're everywhere!' I shouted.

'Fire back!' ordered Wendy, but then she turned and got hit on the helmet twice. From in front of us, a cheer went up. It was Leon's voice. Wendy grinned and sat down.

'Be with you in ten,' she told us. 'Go get 'em . . . !'

WHOOSH! WHOOSH!

'Let's get out of here!' shouted Chris as we all went our separate ways.

I crashed through some bushes and down a bank into the water. I stayed on the edge, trying not to get too wet. Suddenly Emma slid down the bank too and appeared at my side.

'Good move!' she told me.

'I just slipped,' I told her. 'I didn't mean to—'

'SSSSHHHH!!!!' she whispered, pointing above her head.

I looked up and saw someone's feet.

'It's Abs,' Emma told me. 'He was chasing me. Let's get him!'

She crawled along the bank until she was behind where Abs was. I went the other way. Slowly we both started to climb the bank. At the top we waited and then, just when Abs least expected it, we jumped up and plastered him with red paint. He must have been hit with five balls.

'That's not fair!' he moaned. 'I wasn't ready . . .'

'Sit down!' replied Emma triumphantly, before giving me a high-five.

'What next?' I asked. 'Where's everyone else?'

'I don't know,' said Emma, 'but we should try to get across the stream. Wendy said to head for the Blue base.'

'Cool!' I said. 'Follow me . . .'

We found the bridge and crossed it without seeing anyone else from the Blues. But we didn't spot anyone from our team either. And I suddenly realized we didn't have a radio with us.

'We'll have to find Chris or Mr Singh,' said Emma.

'They'll be heading for the Blue base too,' I told her. 'Why don't we just meet them there?'

'OK,' she said. 'Do you know where to go?'

The problem was that we didn't have a map either. I looked straight ahead, which was north, and then off to the left a little bit.

'Mr Singh said to go north-west,' I explained. 'So . . . *this* way.' I nodded towards another spinney that was thick with dark and twisted trees. It looked really spooky.

'After you,' Emma told me, looking a bit worried.

'I've got those stickers,' I told her. 'We'll stick them to the trees just in case we get lost.'

'Just like Hansel and Gretel,' she replied.

I pulled out the stickers and stuck one to the first tree we reached. Now we couldn't lose ourselves and go missing . . .

Chapter 7

Half an hour later it had started raining again and we were lost.

'I said we should have turned right!' protested Emma.

'We did!' I replied, getting annoyed.

We'd turned right and left and right again and it was still no use. No matter what we did we just found ourselves deeper and deeper into the spinney. The branches were sopping wet and huge droplets of rainwater were thudding on top of my head.

'Where did we put the last sticker

again?' Emma asked.

'I can't remember,' I told her. 'It was back there somewhere.' I gestured to the left with my head.

'What are we going to do?' she asked.

I thought for a minute. The map that I'd seen hadn't been *that* big. Surely if we just kept going in a straight line we'd come out somewhere. But that was part of the problem. The trees and bushes were *so* dense that we couldn't be sure we were actually moving straight ahead.

'Let's go back the way we've just come,' I said.

'This is like one of those silly movies,' replied Emma.

'What movies?' I asked.

'Silly ones – I just told you. Knowing *our* luck, there's probably some monster lurking in the trees waiting to eat us for dinner,' she moaned.

'Don't be so daft,' I told her.

Suddenly there was a loud cracking sound.

'What was that?' asked Emma with a start.

I spun round to see where the noise had come from, but I couldn't see anything.

'What is it?' Emma asked again.

'Nothing,' I replied. 'Come on . . . let's go this way.'

I led her to the left, away from the noise. I was sure it was nothing but I was still a bit spooked out, mostly because of what Emma had said about silly movies. But they were just films. There was no way there could be anything out there. That was just stupid.

CRASH!!!!!!!!!

'Oh, my God!' shrieked Emma. 'There's something out there!'

This time I was properly scared. Whatever had made the second noise was really close by. I lifted my paint gun and held it in front of myself.

'Let's just go anywhere,' suggested Emma.

'Yeah,' I agreed.

We pushed through some branches and suddenly there was a slight clearing. In the middle was an upturned tree. I walked over to it and sat down.

'What are you doing?' asked Emma.

'I'm thinking,' I told her. 'We haven't been this way before.'

She sat down next to me and sighed.

'Shall we just shout out until someone hears us?' she asked.

'We could,' I replied.

From within the tree-line something moved quickly. It stopped and then it moved again.

'It's nothing,' I told Emma. 'It's probably just a bird or a badger or something.'

'I'm not scared!' said Emma. 'Honest . . .'

'Do you think the others are looking for us?' I asked.

'I hope so,' she replied. 'It would be a bit mean if they weren't.'

'But we've only been gone about an hour,' I said. 'Gavin said the course normally takes a few hours . . .'

Emma looked worried. 'And we've not seen anyone,' she reminded me. 'No one at all . . .'

'I'm sure they've missed us by now,' I replied.

There was some more rustling in the trees. Then another loud crack. And then something began to growl . . .

'Come on!' I shouted, grabbing Emma's hand and running towards the other side of the clearing.

Emma screamed and followed me. We pushed our way through more trees, and then suddenly my feet slipped from beneath me and I went crashing down a steep bank with Emma right behind me. We ended up knee-deep in the stream. The water was freezing.

'*Eurghh!!!!!!!!!!*' moaned Emma.

Something moved along the top of the bank.

'It's still there,' I said. 'Let's just follow the stream.'

'But I'm wet!' she complained.

'It doesn't matter,' I told her. 'Let's go . . .'

Whatever was up on the bank moved again and then there was another growling sound. Only it was deeper than the first one.

'I'm scared!' Emma told me.

'So am I,' I admitted.

Whoosh! *WHOOSH! WHOOSH!* The water around us turned blue and then red. And then someone started giggling. Someone else started laughing. The third person

sounded like they were almost *crying* with laughter. I looked up the steep bank and saw them: Chris, Abs and Lily!

'What are you doing?' I demanded. 'Chris! Lily! We're supposed to be on the same side!'

'GOTCHA!!!!!!!!!!!!' shouted Abs, before splattering me with blue paint balls.

'You nasty, horrible, nasty . . . horrible idiots!' shouted Emma.

She didn't get to say anything else because Lily blasted her with paint too. Red paint . . .

When we got back to everyone else, I wasn't bothered about who'd won the challenge. I was cold and wet and my feet hurt. But I wasn't as bad as our goalkeeper, Gurinder, who had tripped and twisted his ankle. It was really badly swollen and it was obvious that he wasn't going to be able to play in our next game. His dad had taken him to the hospital to get his ankle x-rayed.

Lily was excited because Gurinder's injury meant that our reserve keeper, Gem, would get a game.

'She's brilliant!' Lily told anyone who would listen.

I looked around at the squad. The Blue team had officially won and no one from our side was even complaining. It was strange because everyone was just having a laugh together – boys *and* girls. It looked like the coaches had been right to bring us on this team-bonding exercise. And *everyone* had cheered loudly when Emma arrived back and blasted Gavin with one paint ball after another!

'OK, people!' shouted Wendy. 'Time to go home. Training on Thursday this week, although we'll be around on Tuesday too, for anyone who wants to do extra. Hope you had a good time and bring on the next game!'

'YEAH!!!!!!!!!!!!!!' we all shouted.

My mum walked over to me and gave me a hug.

'Mum!' I complained, trying to get away.

'Oh – don't be like that, Jason! Give your mummy a hug . . .' she said.

'Yeah, Jason,' Parvy said to me, with a huge grin. 'Give Mummy a huggy-wuggy!'

My face went red as Parvy, Lily, Chris and Abs started laughing at me. Dal didn't laugh. Instead he gave me a shrug.

'Parents . . .' he said, just as his dad walked over and complained about losing.

'That was all a set-up!' Mr Singh said.

'Dad!'

'Well – it was!' he continued. 'There was no way I was shot three times . . . !'

'It's only a game, Dad!' Dal reminded him.

'Don't care!' replied Mr Singh like a spoiled little kid. 'Your team cheated!'

I grinned at Dal. 'You reckon it's easy to swap your parents for some less annoying?' I asked.

'Hope so,' joked Dal.

'Come on!' said my mum. 'Let's go home.'

Chapter 8

Saturday

By the time I got to the match against Rockwell Rangers, everyone else had already arrived. My mum had made me late, waiting for a plumber to turn up and sort out our washing machine.

'I'm ever so sorry,' she said to Wendy as we walked in.

'It's no problem,' Wendy replied. 'Just let us know if possible.' She turned to me. 'Go and get changed, Jason,' she told me. 'The rest of the team are out there already, so be quick.'

I nodded.

'Sorry, son,' my mum said for about the hundredth time that morning.

''S OK,' I reassured her. 'We had to get the machine fixed.'

I ran into the boys' changing room and got ready, just before the Rangers players turned up. I was pulling on my boots when they walked in. They were talking about a television crew they'd seen arrive in a TV-company van.

'Wonder why *they're* here?' asked one of the lads.

'Dunno,' said his mate. 'But they look like they're going to film the game.'

'It's because our team is different,' I told them as I finished tying my laces.

They both looked at me.

'Why?' asked the first boy.

'Haven't you heard?' I replied with a smile.

'We've got girls playing for us and they're brilliant!'

I might as well have told them we had elephants playing for us – they both looked so shocked.

'You're joking with us, aren't you?' asked the first one.

I shook my head. 'See you on the pitch,' I said as I walked out past the rest of the Rangers team.

'They've got girls in their side!' I heard one of the lads say to the rest.

'We'll definitely beat them now!' said another. 'And we'll be on the telly when we do it – brilliant!'

'You wish,' I said under my breath.

We may have had a bad start to the season but I had a funny feeling that things were about to get better. I don't know why, but something inside me told me that we were going to beat Rockwell Rangers.

Our squad was getting together for the team talk when I got outside. And Abs and Chris were arguing with each other.

'Potato head!' Abs said to Chris.

'Doughnut!' replied Chris.

'You're the doughnut,' answered Abs.

'And you kick the ball like a girl!'

'Abs!' said Parvy, Gem, Lily and Emma at the same time.

'Sorry,' he replied sheepishly. 'I meant rubbish girls – not you lot, honest.'

'Ahhh,' said Chris. 'Look at Abs and the Barbies . . . they love you!'

'No!'

'Yeah!'

'No!'

'Yeah!'

'Oh, please be quiet!' said Wendy.

'Yes, miss,' they both said together.

'And call me Wendy,' she went on.

As we gathered together, Ian and Steve went through who was playing where. It was the same team as the last game except for three changes. Firstly, Gem was in goal for the injured Gurinder, and secondly Ant was playing instead of Corky, who had a cold but was there anyway.

'You're going to give us your germs!' moaned Emma.

'Won't,' replied Corky.

'Will!' said Emma.

'WON'T!'

'WILL!'

Ian blew his whistle.

'Button it!' he demanded. 'The final change is Jason.'

I looked up in shock. What did he mean by saying I was the final change? Wasn't I in the team today?

'We're going to give Emma a run-out today so, Jason, you're a sub, OK?' he told me.

He must have read my face because he
continued, 'It's nothing personal, son. We
just think it's fair if we give some of the
other players a chance. And you will come
on at some point, OK?'

I nodded. I was really disappointed, but I
didn't want to act like a baby. Ian was right
about giving everyone a chance. I just wished
it wasn't me that was being replaced. Was it
because I'd turned up late . . . ?

'Right, Rushton – get out there and show
them what you're made of!' shouted Steve.
'And remember the weekend. We are a
TEAM!'

'YEAH!' shouted Byron and Leon.

'Let's go!' added Dal.

I walked to the sideline as the team took
up their positions. That was when I saw the
camera crew for the first time. I'd forgotten
what the Rangers players had said in the
changing room because of hearing that I

wasn't playing. Now the camera was only fifteen metres up the line from where I was standing.

Wendy came up to me just as I wanted to ask her about the filming.

'Are you OK, Jason?' she asked me.

I nodded.

'It's not because you did badly or anything,' she said. 'You're one of our star players. It's just that . . .'

''S OK, miss,' I replied.

She grinned. 'Wendy . . .' she reminded me again.

'Oh, yeah,' I said, before nodding at the film crew. 'Are they your mates then?' I asked her.

She nodded. There were two men and a woman in the crew. One man held a camera with a built-in microphone and the other one had a clipboard. Next to them was a lady with long blonde hair wearing posh-looking clothes.

'They're going to watch the game and ask some questions,' Wendy told me. 'They are really excited by our mixed team and they are thinking of making a documentary if they like what they see today.'

'Really?' I asked, getting a little excited.

'Yes. I think they'll be chatting to the subs soon so you might even get on the telly if they end up using any of today's footage.'

'Cool!' I replied.

Chapter 9

The game kicked off five minutes later and immediately Rockwell Rangers were on the attack. They were passing the ball really well but at one point, just as he was about to intercept, Byron slipped, missed his challenge and they were bearing down on our defence.

But then Emma came flying in from her position and took the ball away from one of their players. The lad went flying as Emma took him out too, but the ref saw it as a foul and gave Rangers a direct free kick just outside our box.

'REF!' shouted Dal's dad from the sidelines. 'That was a clean tackle.'

The ref shook his head and walked up to Emma. He had a few words with her and then the Rangers' captain, who was called Michael, placed the ball. He took three steps back and then tried to curl the ball over our wall into the top corner of the goal. But Gem was equal to it and she sprang into action, palming the ball away for a corner.

Steven and Dal congratulated her as Rangers lined up for the corner kick. The ball was soon back in our box but this time Emma won it fairly and ran with it, out of the box and across to the left, where she played it to Ant.

Inside Ant was Abs, who screamed for a pass – which he got. He twisted to his right and then he was away. Two Rangers players tried to keep up with him but Abs is quite fast and he just outran them. Lily was making a darting run inside the Rangers' left back and Abs saw her.

He played a lovely ball through to her which she took in her stride. She stepped across it twice and then pushed it into a space inside the Rangers' box. I strained to see who was there as I hadn't noticed anyone making a run for her. But then Leon popped up, even though he's our right back, and he smashed the ball towards goal. But the shot was off target and the game restarted with a goal kick for Rangers.

Ten more minutes went by as the game reached a high tempo, with either us or Rangers on the attack. It was what football commentators call an 'open game', and on the sidelines Ian was going mental, shouting at our midfield to stop Rangers passing the ball.

'Get tight to them!' he called out. 'Get your foot in!'

I was urging the team on and didn't notice that the camera crew had walked up to my side. It was only when the lady tapped me on the shoulder that I realized. I turned to find the camera in my face and the lady smiling at me in a weird way.

'I understand you had to make way for one of the girls today?' she asked me, in the same way that TV reporters ask questions.

I nodded, worried about the camera. What was I going to say and who was going to see it? And then my mum suddenly appeared at my side, smoothing down my hair with her palm.

'*Mum!*' I complained.

'Never mind, poppet,' she said annoyingly. 'You need to look your best for the camera.'

And then she pretty much shoved me

out of the way and started answering the question for me.

'Of course, my son Jason is one of the star players,' she told the woman, 'but he's been playing ever so regularly and he needed a rest so the coaches went for squad rotation and . . .'

My mum sounded like she was presenting *Match of the Day*. I couldn't believe what she was saying. She didn't have a clue what she was talking about. I remember once trying to explain the offside rule to her during a Chelsea versus Liverpool game, and she actually fell asleep and started snoring.

'And is that how you see it, Jason?' asked the lady with the camera crew.

'Er . . . well, I don't mind,' I told her. 'Emma – that's the girl who's playing for me – she's really good, and besides, we are a team,' I said.

That's when the Rangers team erupted

with joy. I'd been so busy with the camera crew that I'd stopped watching the game and now Rangers had scored.

It was 1–0!

'MUM!!!!!!!!!!!!!!!' I moaned.

'What is it, poppet?'

'Oh – don't call me that!' I added. Walking off up the touchline, I wished I could walk into where she worked and embarrass her too, just like she did with me. Parents!

Chapter 10

We were still 1–0 down at half-time and as the second half started, Steve and Wendy told me and Penny to get warmed up. Penny was an attacker and I wondered whether that meant that one of my friends, Abs or Chris, would be coming off. I knew that neither of them would be pleased if they did.

As I was thinking this, Rangers scored again.

'OH, NO!!!!!!!!!!!!!!!!!' shouted Wendy.

'Come on, *Reds*!!!!!!!!!!!!!!' complained Ian. 'That was silly!'

The team were all looking at each other and complaining – all blaming the other players. Something was wrong, and if we didn't fix it soon we would end up getting thrashed.

'Are you both ready to come on?' Wendy asked me and Penny.

As we'd both been warming up during half-time anyway, both of us nodded. I didn't need to be any warmer. I was just itching to get onto the pitch.

'Right then,' said Ian. 'You're on!'

Ian shouted to Steven and called him over.

'We're going four-three-three,' he told him once he'd jogged across. 'And I want Leon and Parvy to push on too. Squeeze the middle of the park and get in their faces!'

'Yes, coach,' Steven nodded.

I waited for Wendy to tell the ref about the substitutions as Steve and Ian spoke to each other. They were pointing at the pitch and gesturing with their hands. Steve looked like he was conducting an orchestra. Then he came up to me and Penny.

'Bill Shankly . . .' he began.

'Who?' both of us asked in confusion.

'Famous old manager . . . never mind who he is – just listen. He used to tell his players to take the ball into the opposition's half and dare them to take it away. That's what I want. Take the game to Rangers. Don't give them time to think. Pass, move, pass, move!!'

'OK,' I replied.

The players being replaced were Ant and Emma. Penny went on and joined Chris and Abs up front and I went on into midfield. It was a risk because we only had three players in midfield now – me, Lily and Byron – to

Rangers' four. But with our full backs, Leon and Parvy, pushing up, it started to work in our favour.

As soon as the game restarted we were better as a team. Byron was playing in front of Dal and Steven – our central defenders – and Leon and Parvy were like extra midfielders. Lily was doing her thing out on the wing and I played on the other side. Rangers didn't know what had hit them.

The ball was at Byron's feet and he squared it to Lily, who went on one of her jinking runs towards the Rangers defence. Just as she was about to get tackled she did her little *ninja* trick, as she called it. In one movement, she lifted the ball and knocked it on, leaving the defender stranded and looking sheepish. I have no idea how she did the move — I couldn't do it — but it didn't matter. Lily was bearing down on the Rangers goal with Chris and Penny in great positions. She waited though, and instead of passing to Chris or Penny, she played the ball behind them to Abs.

The Rangers defence were wrong-footed and Abs slotted the ball home calmly.

Goal! Abs was on target today — making up for missing that penalty in the last match.

2–1.

No one in our team celebrated. Instead we all ran back to our positions, ready to get on with our comeback. We'd caught up one goal, but we needed one more at least . . .

'COME ON, YOU REDS!!!!!' came the cry from the supporters.

Rangers had a couple of minutes of possession before we got the ball back. For the next fifteen minutes, we began wave after wave of attacks on their goal, but we didn't score.

Then Rangers had a great chance, one on one with our keeper Gem, but Byron got back in time and robbed the ball from one of their strikers, just as he was about to shoot. Within three passes we were back on the attack!

Parvy ran down the left wing and then turned, passing across to me. I looked up and saw two Rangers players coming for me. I sidestepped one and passed to Abs. Then I sprinted into the space that had been left by the defender. Abs chipped the ball to Chris, who ran at his defender. The lad he was running towards looked scared and Chris soon had the better of him.

He played the ball right to Lily, who was totally outplaying her defender. She skipped past him for the tenth time and crossed towards Penny, who was facing the goal.

But there were two players in front of her and she didn't have a clean shot. I was running up behind her, screaming for a pass. I expected her to turn but she didn't. Instead, cool as a cucumber, she back-heeled the ball into my path.

I thought about placing the ball either side of the Rangers goalie but then I made up my mind to blast it. I caught it perfectly and it flew into the net like a rocket.

2–2!

'YESSSSSSSSSSSSSSSSSSSSSSSSSS!!!!!!!!!!!!!!!!!' I shouted.

Once we had regrouped, Ian bellowed out at us to let us know we had just five minutes left to play.

'Five minutes to grab victory from defeat! COME ON, REDS!' screamed Wendy.

'Come on, poppet!' added my mum.

I ignored her. Instead I had to chase back after the Rangers captain, Michael, who was making a dangerous run. I caught him just outside our box and I managed to nick the ball from his feet. I turned with it and played it down the wing to Lily.

Once again she set off, twisting left and right and making her defender dizzy. Once she'd teased him enough she pushed the ball past him and accelerated like a sports car. She was heading for the touchline and I was certain she'd kicked the ball too far. There was no way she was going to catch it. But then Lily did something absolutely amazing. She kept the ball in play. Then she turned to see a defender in front of her. He was huge and he was almost growling as he ran towards her.

Calmly, she put the ball through his legs, ran around him and then switched inside. This gave her a much better angle to shoot at the goal. I thought she'd go with her left foot but she didn't. Instead she curled it with the outside of her right foot.

The ball sailed in a wide arc and then turned at the last minute like a missile. The Rangers goalie tried his best to get to it but he couldn't. The ball pinged off the far post and fell into the net.

3–2!

Our entire team ran after Lily, whooping and cheering as she celebrated by diving to the ground with her arms out wide. She slid through mud and grass, getting filthy dirty, but I don't think she cared. It was an amazing goal.

Don't miss any of the titles in this action-packed
football series!

Available now:

Bali Rai

SOCCER SQUAD

★ STARTING ELEVEN

**'Come on!' I shouted to my team-mates.
'Let's start playing!'**

The local youth club are putting an under-elevens
squad together – and Dal, Chris, Abs and Jason are
determined to be picked. They know they're the best
players in their school – but what if that isn't good
enough and they don't make the team? Dal knows
he'd be gutted if his mates made it and he didn't . . .

The first in a fantastic new football series from an
author with real street cred!

978 1 862 30654 7

ABOUT THE AUTHOR

Bali Rai thinks he is a very lucky man. He gets to write all day if he wants to, or to go into schools to speak to his readers about what they think of his books. He loves films, music, reading, seeing friends and watching his beloved Liverpool FC.

Bali played for his school team as a defender and loved it. He has been a lifelong football fan since he began watching *Match of the Day* at the age of four with his dad. He enjoys talking and arguing about Liverpool FC and would like to be Rafa Benitez's or Steven Gerrard's personal servant, but if this does not happen he is happy to carry on writing for his thousands of fans.

Bali was very honoured that his short novel *Dream On* (about a young footballer) was chosen for the first Booked-Up list and was made available to every Year 7 school child.

Bali's books are now in ten languages and he also gets to travel all over the world to meet his readers. He hopes that he can encourage anyone to have a go at writing and to find a love of reading. He has won lots of book awards and really enjoys winning the ones that are voted for by the real readers – you!

Bali lives in his home city of Leicester. He has a lovely new wife and a football-crazy daughter.

One by one we did the same celebration. We hadn't planned it though – everyone was just copying Lily. And the camera guy was filming every minute of it, especially with Lily and the rest of the girls. By the time the final whistle blew we were all covered in mud and as happy as we'd ever been.

We'd just won our first game of the season and it felt great! After missing chances in our first games, today we were bang on target – hitting the back of the net three times! Now we were ready to step up and win our next game too. And then who knew where we'd be – cup winners, even the league! All I knew was that the other teams needed to watch out. The Reds were on the up!